Dragon's Hoard
NomNoms Vol. 2

edited by
Dreamous

**ADULT
READERS
ONLY**

DRAGON'S HOARD:
NOMNOMS VOLUME 2

Copyright © 2013
by Rabbit Valley
All rights reserved

Published by
Rabbit Valley Comics
Flagstaff, Arizona
https://www.rabbitvalley.com

ISBN 978-1-62475-027-4

Printed in the United States,
United Kingdom, or Australia
First printing June 2013
Second printing January 2022

Cover art by Demonic
Compendium
Interior art by DarkNatasha,
Sidian, SkullDog, SalirethS,
Eendris, Jace, NecroDrone

Table of Contents

Front Cover by Demonic Compendium

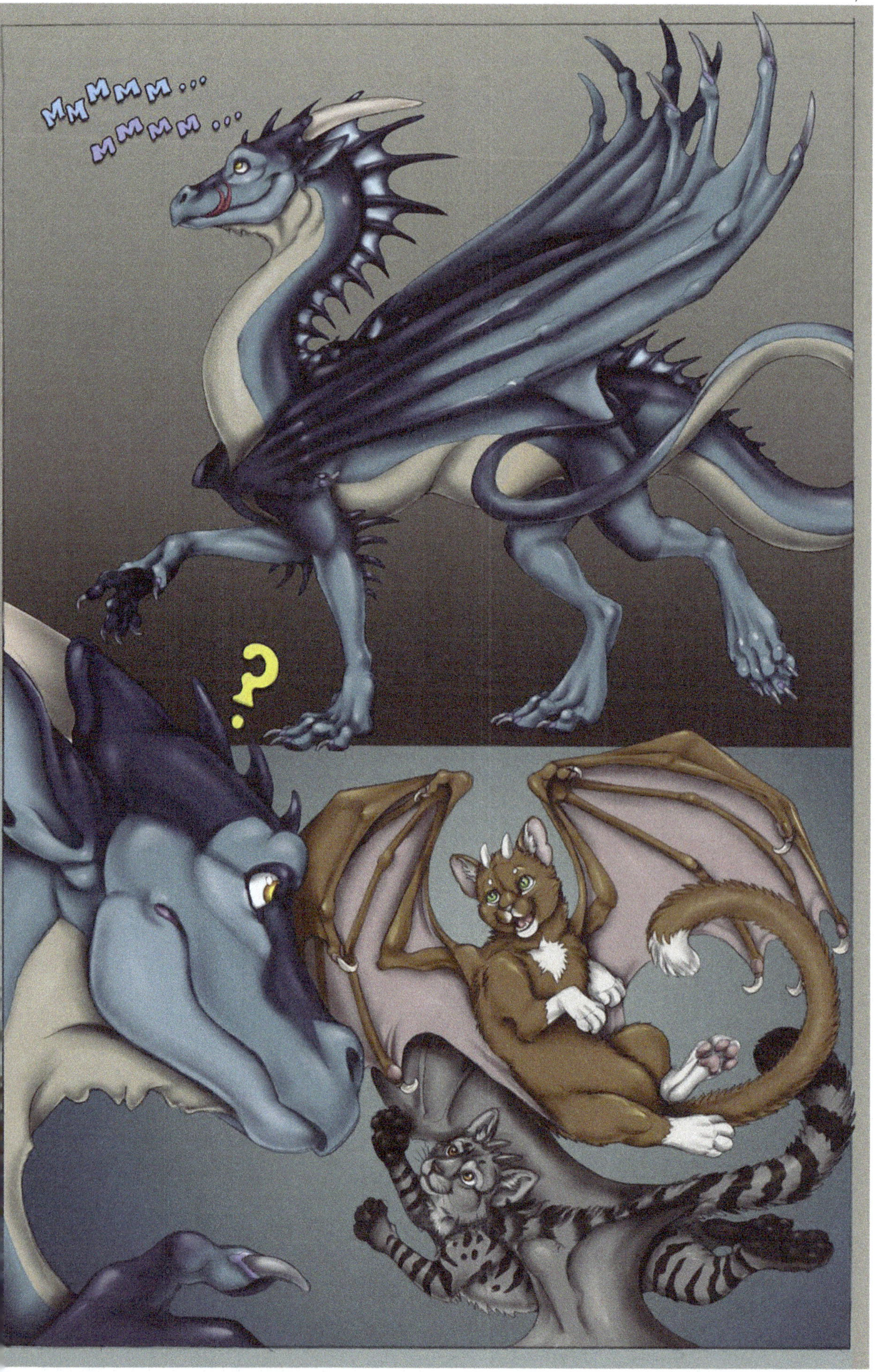
MMMMM...
MMMMM...
?

10

SHHSCK

GHH--

MMM-

MMM-

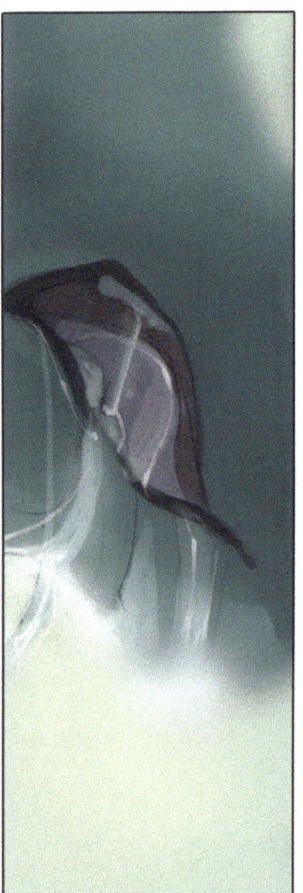

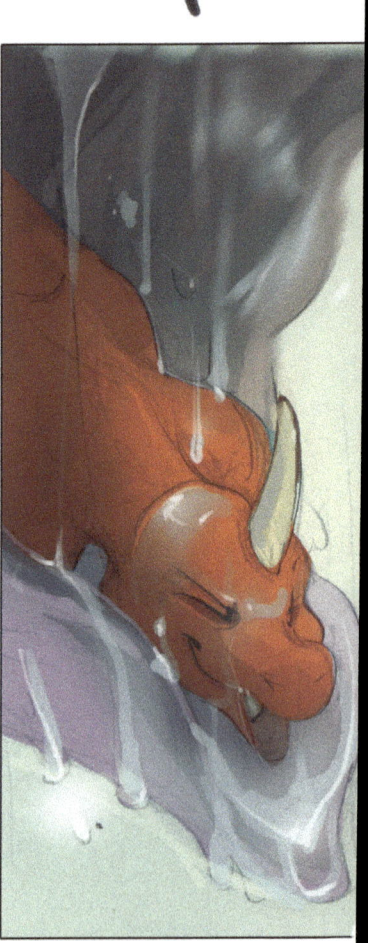

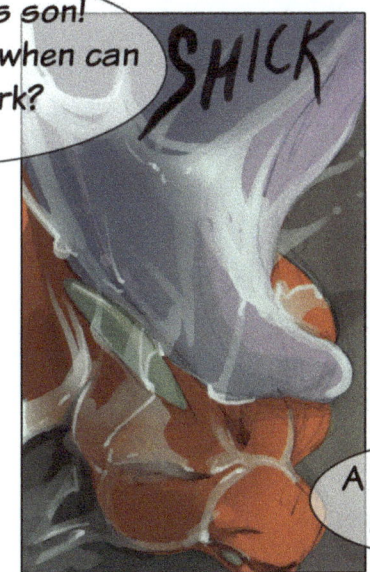

I AM LISTENING
TO OUR
QUIET BREATH

A SHORT COMICS
BY THE DIMENSONAL TRAVELLER *SALIRETHS*
AND THE MYSTERIOUS EENDRIS
SPECIAL THANKS FOR
THE MAGNIFICENT DRAKKOR
AND PATIENT FRIENDS

Location: Hsar'Xagaths planet
          Archstone Islands
Timeplane: Uknown

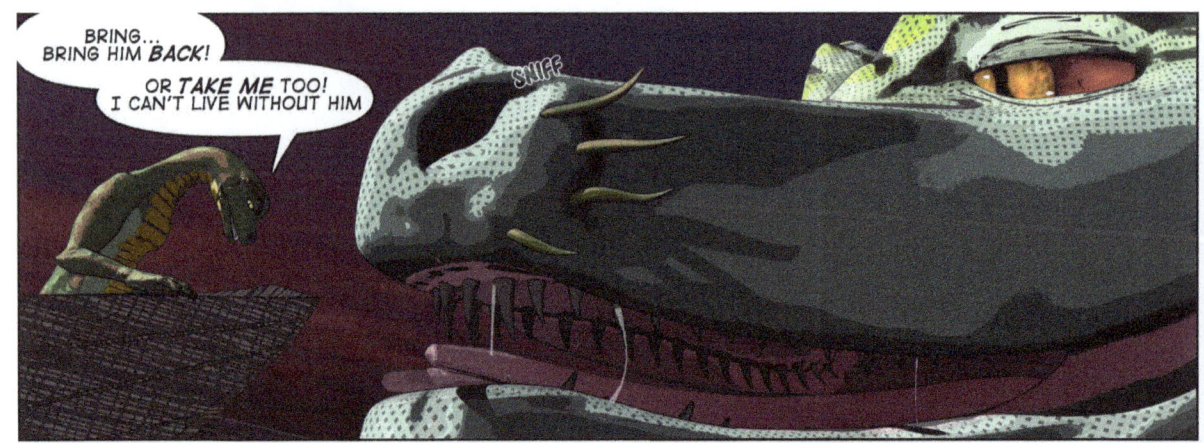

23

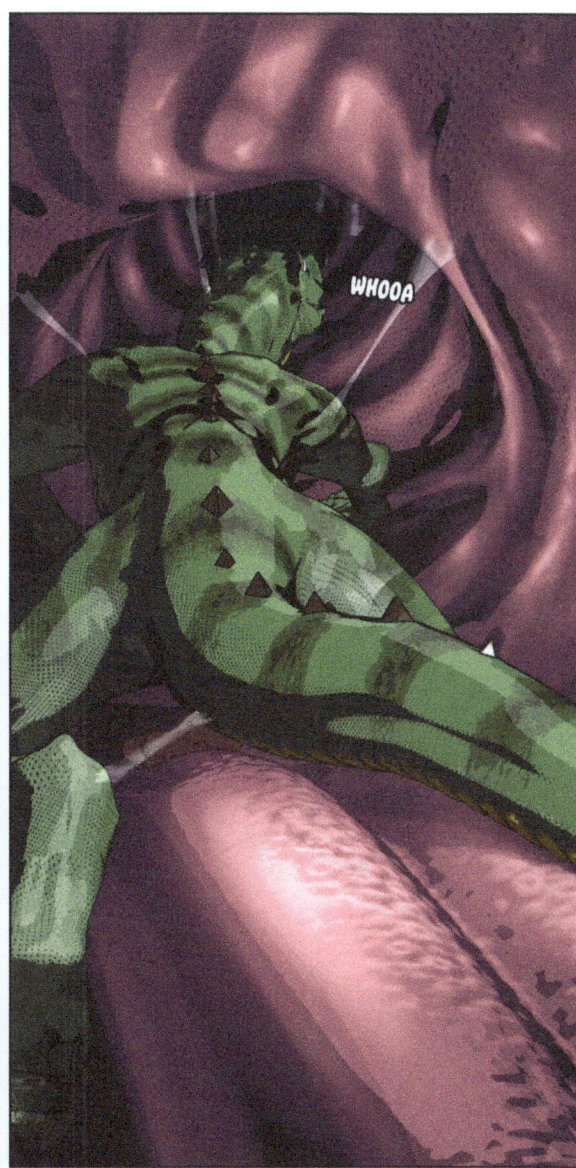

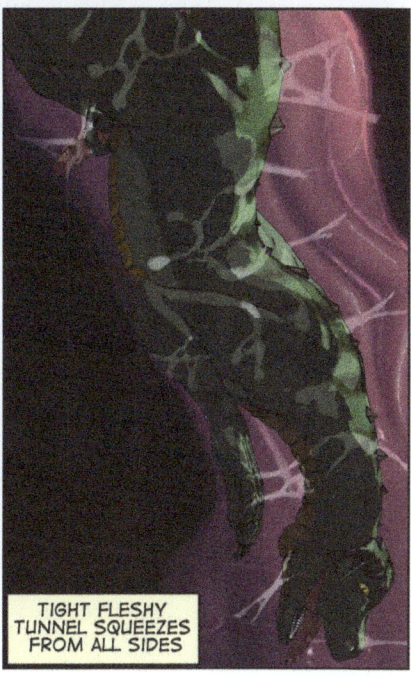

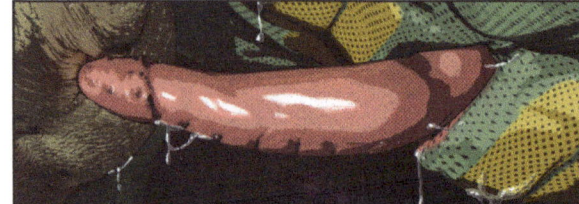

THE END

32

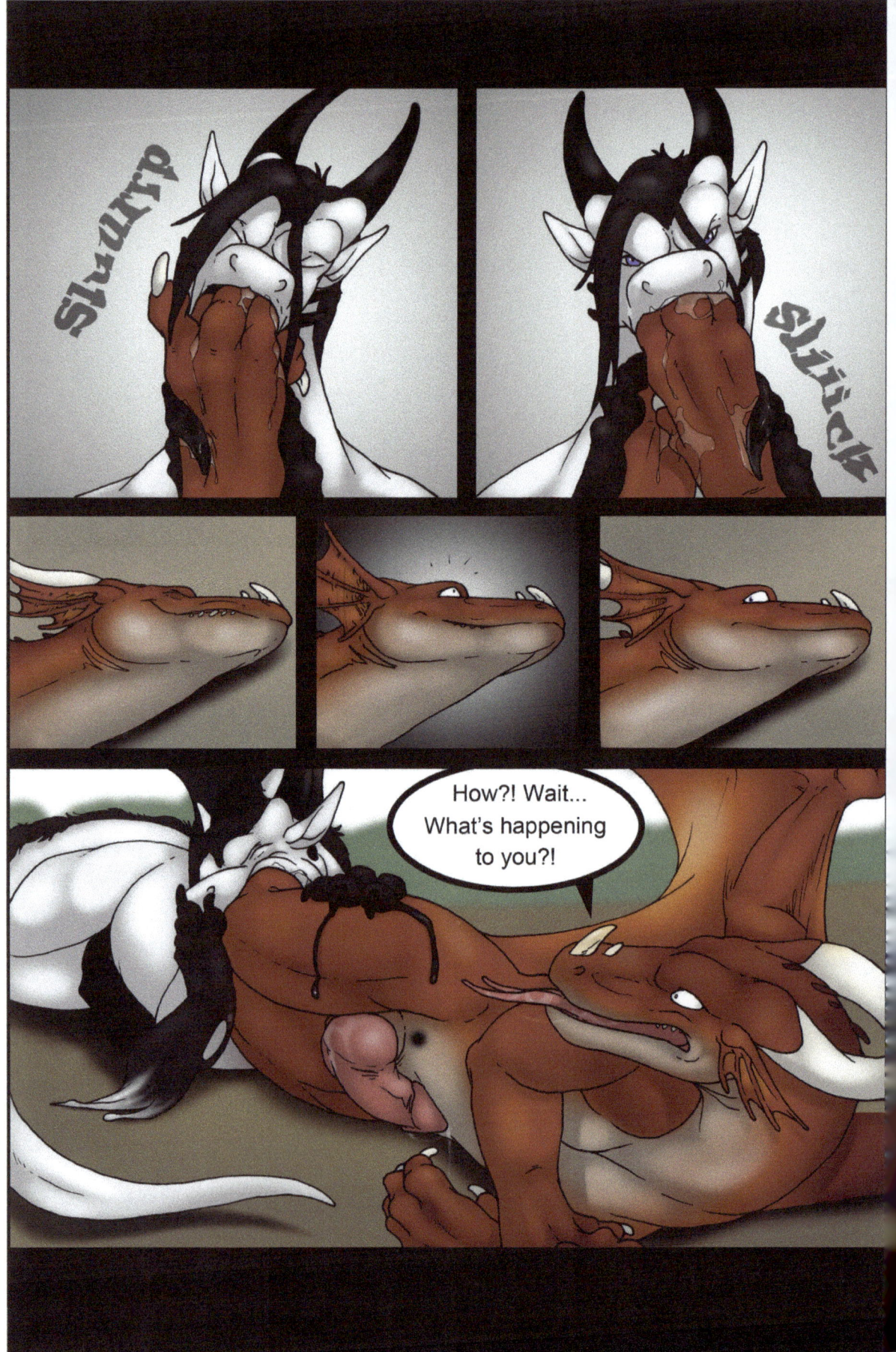

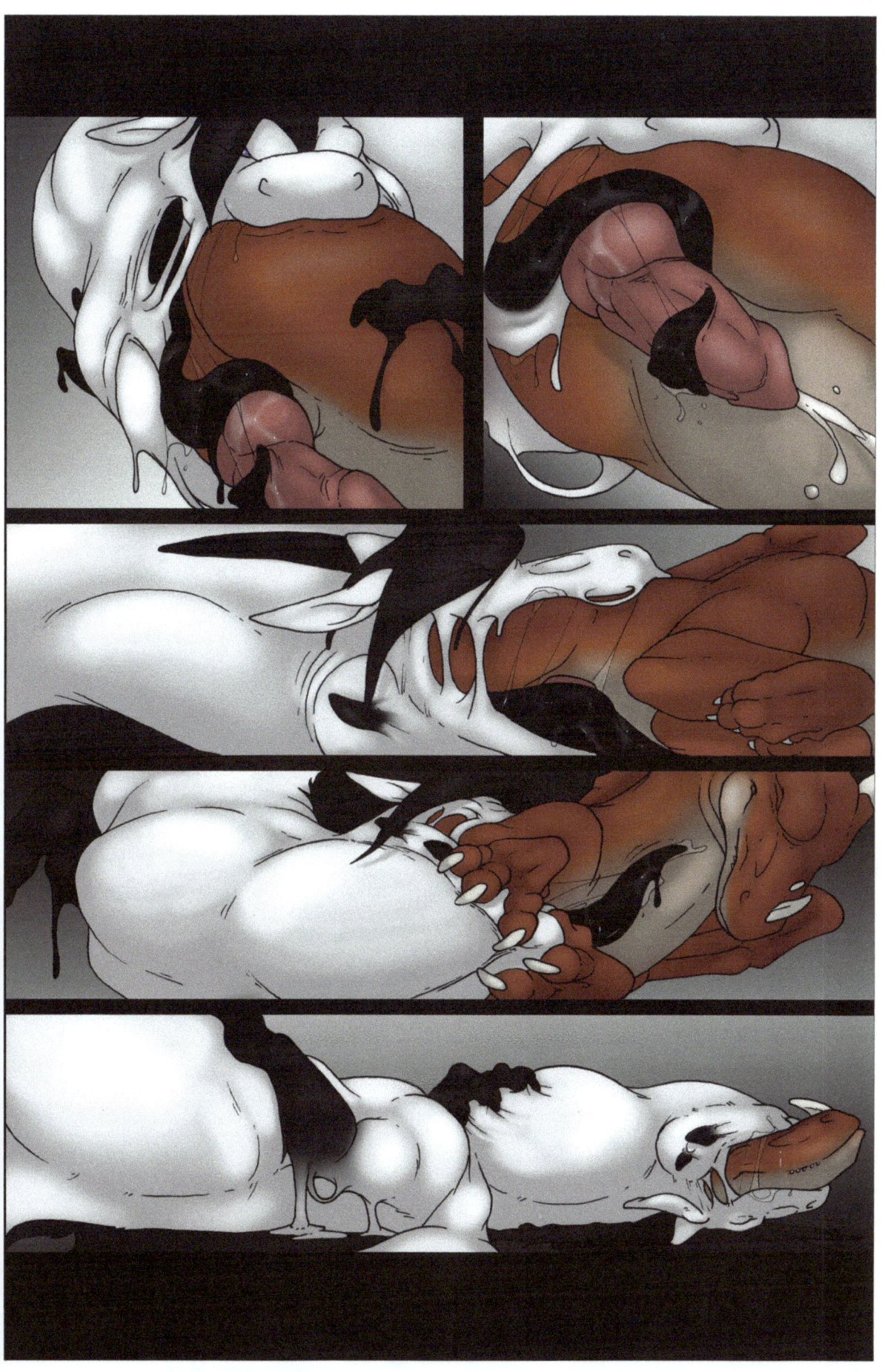

Danger: Choking Hazard - Runt Volume One
Available at RabbitValley.com

Can't eat just one... - Runt Volume Two
Available at RabbitValley.com

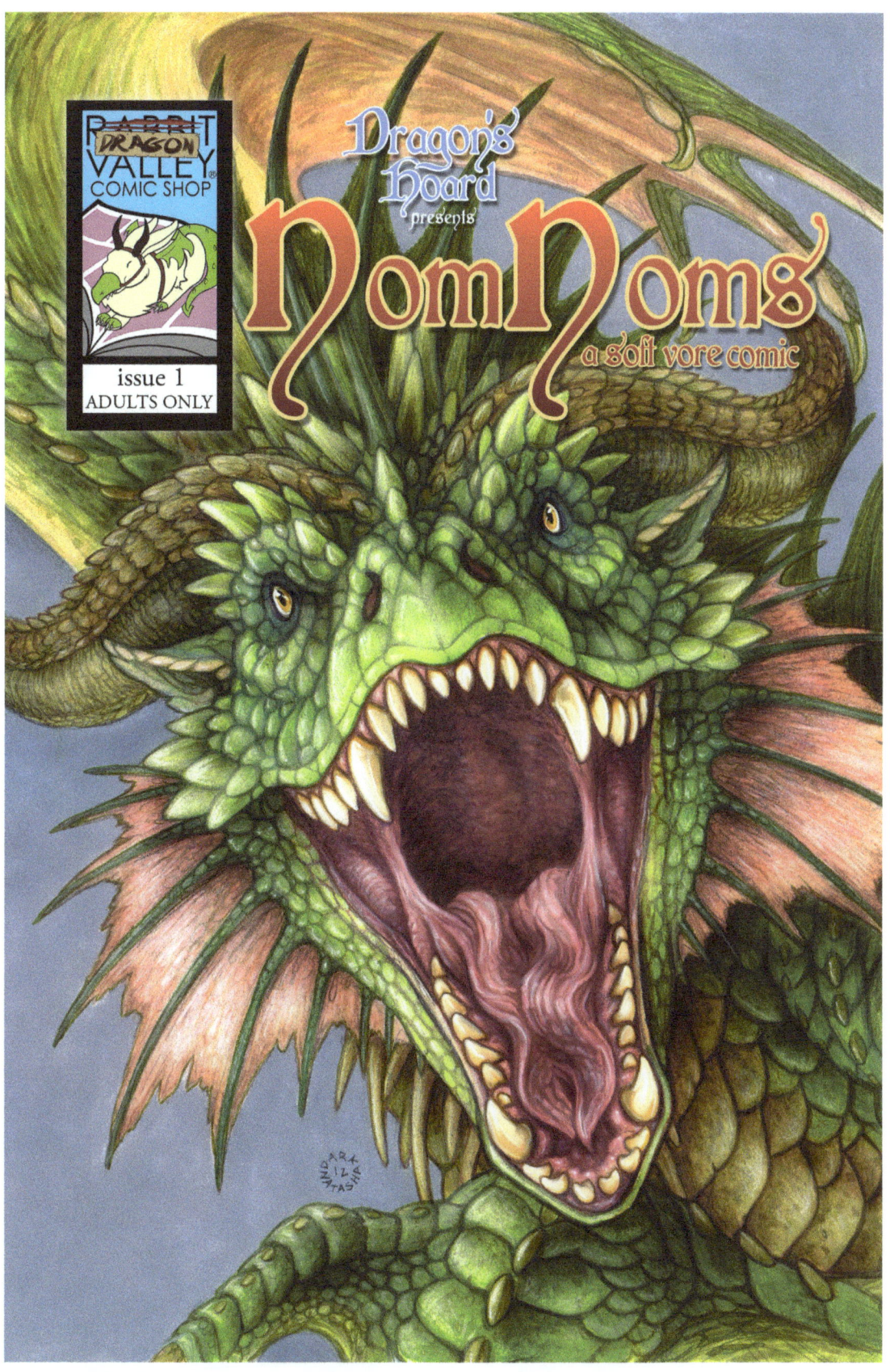

Stay Hungry, My Friends - NomNoms Volume 1
Available at RabbitValley.com

A note from **Spire**:

My fellow ravenous dragons and ravenous dragon fans,

Thank you for once again supporting our work. The delectable delights found in this book are only made possible through the patronage of our fans (and boy, do I ever appreciate that these comics are possible!). The continued contribution of our dedicated fans has made Dragon's Hoard into quite the comic entity, now 8 titles strong! Even more so, all our fans' insatiable appetite for voracious work has allowed NomNoms to become a running title, now scheduled to publish a new comic yearly! I couldn't be happier to see what started as a tasty little idea become a full fledged banquet of delight.

Though I've said it before, I cannot express strongly enough what all your patronage means to me. Seeing my small idea become something so big, often topping the popularity charts at Rabbit Valley, means so very much to me. I will strive to bring more works of this quality and content to sate all those draconic desires your lusty hearts have.

And finally, a tidbit of of advice - Don't over-season your gryphon! Let their natural, rich, delicious, lucious taste be the focus of your meal! ... I need to go find Ruse now. Until next comic!

...

squawk

If you like **Dragon's Hoard**, please check out our other titles coming **soon**:

Dragon's Hoard Presents: Runt vol. 2 - A comic by NecroDrone:
Continuing the biology and social interactions of a feral dragon race. The comic focuses upon a Runt, full-grown and elder than many and his interactions with his loving peers in ritual and in bed.
Features: size play, dominance and submission, multiple fetishes, multiple genders

Dragon's Hoard Presents: D.W.A.G.S. vol. 2 - A compilation featuring:
Dragons Who Advocate Gryphon Submission, one of the most base desires (and a personal favorite for this dragon!) amongst our community-that sacred bond of dragon on gryphon love.
Features: feral dragon on gryphons, multiple genders

Dragon's Hoard Presents: Sacrifice - A comic by Spelunker Sal:
Follow the journey of a young hare who forms an unexpected bond with his captor.
Featured: feral dragon on anthro hare, male on male

Dragon's Hoard volume 4 - The classic collection of general feral dragon erotica returns again for another installment!
Featured: feral dragons on feral dragons & various anthros, multiple genders

Sincerely and Lovingly,

(THE EVER HORNY)

DragonsHoardComic@gmail.com
furaffinity.net/user/dragonshoard

goo.gl/5NbQC

www.ingramcontent.com/pod-product-compliance
Lightning Source LLC
Chambersburg PA
CBHW040324250626
47171CB00010B/39